Little Red
and the Kesh Kayl

The Armenian Version of Little Red Riding Hood

Written by
Talene Dadian White

In Memory of Granny

ISBN: 1456518321
ISBN-13: 9781456518325
LCCN: 2011900100
Armeniankidsbooks.com

Once upon a time, there lived a little Armenian girl named *Anoosh*, who was sweet and innocent and loved by everyone. Anoosh was more often called Little Red Hood, or *Garmir Klghanotz*, because of the fiery red hood she always wore. This little hood was made special for Anoosh by her dear *Medz Mayreeg*. The red cloth was sewn with the strength of Medz Mayreeg's hands but made magical by the love in Medz Mayreeg's heart, as you will see ...

One morning, Little Red Hood was playing *tavlou* with her brother *Aram* when Mama called to her and said, "Little Red Hood, Medz Mayreeg is sick with a cold. Can you bring her some of this fresh *lamajun*?"

"Yes, Mama," answered Little Red Hood happily, as she always looked forward to a visit with Medz Mayreeg.

Mama gave Little Red Hood a *bacheeg* and said, "Please remember to stay on the path in the *Shikahogh Forest*. Do not speak with strangers along the way, *ge hasgenas*?"

"Yes, Mama, I understand." Little Red Hood fastened her hood with a bow under her chin. Then, she took hold of the lamajun basket and set out for Medz Mayreeg's house.

Meanwhile, there was a *kesh kayl* living in the forest, who had caught the scent of the delicious lamajun baking in Mama's oven. Lamajun was the kayl's favorite thing to eat. He often prowled around the local lamajun store to steal a bite. But on this day, he followed the scent of the lamajun directly to Little Red Hood.

Little Red Hood was skipping merrily through the Shikahogh Forest, swinging her basket and humming along the way. Suddenly, she heard footsteps approaching. Little Red Hood stopped and looked around but saw nothing suspicious. So, she continued walking, when all of sudden, the kesh kayl jumped out from behind a tree.

The kayl had a long, muscular body, with thick, black fur, sharp claws, and dagger-like teeth. He slowly circled Little Red Hood, gazing fiercely at the lamajun basket and twitching his nose for a better sniff. "Mmmm ... Is that lamajun I smell?" growled the kayl.

"Um, yes," replied Little Red Hood, unsure what to do or say. She had never seen a kayl before, as they were rare in this part of the woods. The poor girl did not know what a wicked animal he was and that it was dangerous to speak with him.

"Lamajun is my favorite," snarled the kayl as he nudged the basket with his long snout.

"Well, I am sorry, but this lamajun was made special for my Medz Mayreeg. She is very sick and I must bring it to her."

"And where does your Medz Mayreeg live?" pried the hungry kayl.

"On the other side of the Shikahogh Forest, the first house in the village, near the *yegeghetsi*."

The kayl crept closer to Little Red Hood, drooling over the thought of snatching and eating the lamajun, but he dared not, as there were lumberjacks cutting trees nearby. Thinking quickly, he said, "Oh, look at all the delicious *dziraner* growing in these trees. You should pick some for your Medz Mayreeg."

Little Red Hood looked up into the trees and saw the golden, juicy dziraner hanging from the branches. "What a good idea! Medz Mayreeg would love some!" Little Red Hood left the forest path and ran from tree to tree, looking for ripe dziraner. Every time she picked one, she carefully tucked it into the basket and ran deeper and deeper into the forest.

But while Little Red Hood was busy picking dziraner, the kesh kayl secretly followed a shortcut to Medz Mayreeg's house, arriving there before Little Red Hood, and out of sight of the lumberjacks.

The kesh kayl knocked at Medz Mayreeg's door, licking his lips at the thought of a good lamajun meal. But there was no answer, and it was quiet inside. Medz Mayreeg had gone to the *shooga*, even with a terrible cold, because she could not resist the one-day sale on *lavash hatz*.

Since no one was at home, the kesh kayl opened the door and sneaked inside. He knew that Little Red Hood, and the basket of lamajun, would be arriving shortly. So, without delay, he put on Medz Mayreeg's pink *hakoosd* and *kelkharg*, and got into bed, hungrily waiting for Little Red Hood and the lamajun.

Moments later, there was a knock at the door. "Who is it?" asked the kesh kayl, trying to imitate Medz Mayreeg's voice.

"It's Little Red Hood!"

"Come in ..." said the kayl, faking a sickly voice.

Little Red Hood entered the house, smiling cheerfully. "Medz Mayreeg, how are you feeling? I brought you some lamajun and freshly picked dziraner."

"Mmmmmm, the lamajun smells delicious! Bring the basket here so that I can have a taste," begged the kayl.

Little Red Hood came closer to the bed and looked suspiciously at the kayl in the Medz Mayreeg disguise. "Why, Medz Mayreeg, I never noticed what big *aganchner* you have!"
"All the better to hear you with," said the kayl as his paws began reaching for the basket.

Little Red Hood stepped back a bit and examined her grandmother with greater doubt. "Medz Mayreeg, what big *achker* you have!" she said with amazement.

"All the better to see you with," answered the kayl, trying to stay calm.

"B-but Medz Mayreeg," stuttered a confused Little Red Hood, "Your *agraner* are so big too!"

"All the better to *eat your lamajun with!*" exclaimed the kayl. He jumped out of the bed and tore the clothes from his furry body. He stood up on his hind legs, raised his sharp claws, and snarled, "Give me that lamajun!"

"Voch!" screamed Little Red Hood, clutching the lamajun basket tightly.

The kayl lunged towards Little Red Hood, opening his jaws to swallow the basket of lamajun whole, but he only caught the edge of her little red hood in his mouth.

Suddenly, the kayl began yelping, "Agh! Agh!" crying and shaking his jaw as if he had swallowed red-hot coals. It was the little fire-colored hood that had magically burned his tongue, right down to his throat.

The kesh kayl ran for the door, howling in pain, but before he could escape, Medz Mayreeg and the lumberjacks stepped inside and blocked his path. Luckily, Medz Mayreeg heard Little Red Hood's screams on her way home from the shooga and called the lumberjacks for help.

The lumberjacks put the kesh kayl in a cage and drove him far away to Siberia. He spent the rest of his days living in a snow-covered wasteland, where he could never harm anyone or eat lamajun ever again.

Little Red Hood continued to wear that little red hood for all her days, forever protected by Medz Mayreeg's strength and love, as are all Armenian children.

PRONUNCIATION GUIDE

Armenian Letter	Approximate English Equivalent
a	car
b	box
ch	church
d	dog
dz	pronounced like a single consonant
e	met
f	fat
g	got
gh	pronounced like a growl in back of throat, like gargling
h	hat
i	meat
j	jet
k	kick
kh	pronounced like a rasping in back of throat
l	lie
m	mat
n	net
o	or
oo	boot
p	pet
r	rat, but "rolled", as in Spanish
s	sit
sh	shut
t	talk
ts	hits
v	van
y	yes
z	zebra
Zh	measure

GLOSSARY

ACHKER — *Ah-ch-keh-rr* Eyes; Achk for singular eye.

AGANCHNER — *Ah-gah-nch-neh-rr* Ears; Aganch for singular ear.

AGRANER — *Ah-grah-neh-rr* Teeth; Agra for singular tooth.

ANOOSH — *Ah-noosh* Female Armenian name, also meaning "sweet"

ARAM — *Ah-rah* Male Armenian name, meaning "high" or "exalted"

BACHEEG — *Bah-cheeg* Kiss

DZIRANER — *Dzee-rah-neh-rr* Apricots; Dziran for singular apricot.

GARMIR KLGHANOTZ — *Gar-meer Kull-gh-ah-noh-ts* Red Hood

GE HASGENAS? — *Guh-Hah-ss-guh-nah-ss?* Do you understand?

HAKOOSD — *Hah-koost* Dress

KELGHARG — *Kull-ghah-rg* Hat

KESH KAYL — *Keh-sh Ky-ll* Bad wolf

LAMAJUN — *Lah-mah-joon* A popular Armenian food, consisting of a thin crust of round dough, topped with ground meat, vegetables, and spices, also considered Armenian pizza.

LAVASH HATZ	*Lah-vah-sh hah-ts* The staple bread of Armenian cuisine, an extremely thin leavened wrap bread, made from wheat flour.
MEDZ MAYREEG	*Meh-dz My-reeg* Grandmother
SHIKAHOGH FOREST	*Shee-kah-hoh-gh* The Shikahogh State Preserve is Armenia's second largest forest reserve and is located in southern Armenia in the Syunik Province. The Shikahogh reserve is habitat for about eleven hundred species of plants and rare animals, such as the leopard, bear, snowcock, viper, hedgehog, and wolf.
SHOOGA	Shoo-gah Market
TAVLOU	*Tah-v-loo* Backgammon
VOCH	*Voh-ch* No
YEGEGHETSI	*Yeh-geh-gheh-tsee* Church

Made in the USA
Lexington, KY
13 December 2011